CLAUDE
All About Keith

Llyfrgelloedd Caerdydd
www.caerdydd.gov.uk/llyfrgelloedd
Cardiff Libraries
www.cardiff.gov.uk/libraries

CAERDYDD
CARDIFF

BASED ON THE *Alex T. Smith* CLAUDE STORIES
DEVISED FOR TELEVISION BY *Sixteen South*

D0335372

It was a fine morning in Pawhaven and Denzel Pedal was selling everything you might need for a hot, sunny day.

A mummy duck and all her baby ducklings went waddling by. One of Denzel's rubber ducks caught the eye of a *real* little duck who stopped to say hello . . . and got left behind!

TOOT-
TOOT-
TOOT!

Just then, Claude strolled by, practising his hooter.

"I love playing my hooter, Sir Bobblysock,"
he said.

"I know you do, Claude," replied Sir Bobblysock.
"That's why I think it's important that some
other people get a chance to enjoy your playing
just as much as I have all morning . . ."

Claude's hooter made a jolly loud noise!
But not quite as loud as . . .

. . . a baby duck, missing his mummy!

"WAAAAAAAAAH!!!"

"That's an awfully big noise for such a tiny little thing," gasped Sir Bobblysock.

"I wonder what he's doing here all by himself?" said Claude, putting his hands on his hips in an Important Fashion.

Benny Begonia trundled over to see what all the fuss was about.

"Aw," he said. "I think he's lost his mummy. If only there was someone who could take care of him – then I could go and look for his mummy in the park."

Claude's ears wobbled and his tail waggled . . .

His eyebrows wiggled . . .

and in his very best
outdoor voice
he cried –

"I CAN DO THAT!"

"We should give him a nice duck-y name . . . like Keith!"

"Excellent," said Benny. "I'll come and get you when I've found Keith's mummy."

Oh dear. Maybe Benny shouldn't have mentioned the word 'mummy' . . .

"WAAAAAAAAAH!!!"

"Let's go and have a cup of tea at Mr Lovelybuns' café," said Claude.

"Good idea," said Sir Bobblysock, who had never knowingly turned down a fondant fancy.

"I don't think Keith has been in a café before," said Sir Bobblysock.

"You show him what to do, Claude – with your nice manners."

Claude felt VERY important. He tucked the corner of his napkin neatly into his collar. He daintily picked up his sandwich and took a careful bite.

Keith saw what to do and soon he and Claude
were both tucking in like billy-o. But then . . .

Claude got a bit giddy. He took a big bite from his sandwich and . . .

. . . SPLAT!

"WAAAAAAAAAH!!!"

Keith did not like being covered in pickle one little bit!

Mr Lovelybuns was rather alarmed by the noise. It was very loud for a café and his customers were getting terribly upset. "Do something, Claude!" he cried.

"Would it help if I played a tune on my hooter?" Claude asked.

"No, Claude," said Mr Lovelybuns quite firmly. "I think Keith might
need to go for a little walk. Outside."

Claude wasn't sure where to take Keith next. But then he had an idea!
"How about story time at the library? That always cheers me up!"

Keith seemed to like it inside the library. It was cool and quiet and far away from the pickle. Miss Hush, the librarian, was reading a story all about a very, very cross dragon.

Miss Hush asked Claude if he could show everyone what the dragon might look like. Claude straightened his beret and smoothed out his jumper and gave his very best impression.

"ROAAAAAAAAAR!"

Keith's beak wobbled and his eyes brimmed with tears.

"Oh no!" groaned Sir Bobblysock, holding on to his specs. "Here we go again . . ."

"WAAAAAAAAAH!!!"

Miss Hush was alarmed by the noise.
It was awfully loud for a library.

"Do something, Claude!" said Miss Hush in her loudest whisper.

"Would it help if I played a tune on my hooter?" shouted Claude,
over the racket.

"Not in the library, Claude!" said Miss Hush quite firmly.

Sir Bobblysock peered out from behind the cushion where he'd taken refuge. "Think, Claude! What would a duckling really like to do?"

"I know!" said Claude. "Let's take Keith swimming!"

Claude hurried down the street to find Denzel,
and quickly popped the little duckling into
one of his paddling pools.

"Keith seems to like swimming," said Denzel.

"He's taken to it like a duck to water," said Sir Bobblysock.

Claude didn't think Keith would mind if he hopped in for a dip too . . .

SPLAAASH!

Keith blinked.

"Oh no," sighed Sir Bobblysock. "Not again."

"WAAAAAAAAAH!!!"

Everyone was surprised by the noise. It was very loud – even for outside!

Claude was relieved when he saw Benny coming back. "Have you found Keith's mummy?" he asked, hopefully.

"Sorry, Claude," said Benny. "I've looked everywhere but I can't find her."

"I should have just stuck with playing my hooter," said Claude, giving it a little toot.

Toot

Then something extraordinary happened . . .

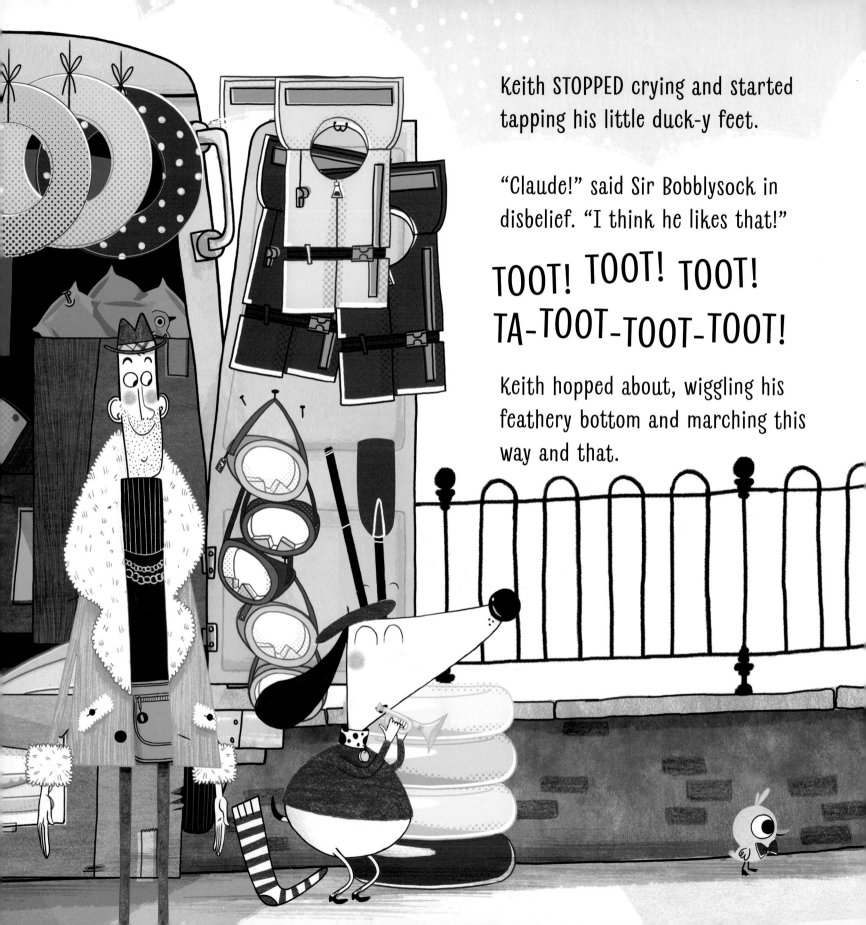

Keith STOPPED crying and started tapping his little duck-y feet.

"Claude!" said Sir Bobblysock in disbelief. "I think he likes that!"

TOOT! TOOT! TOOT! TA-TOOT-TOOT-TOOT!

Keith hopped about, wiggling his feathery bottom and marching this way and that.

And it turned out he wasn't the only one who liked Claude's hooter tooting!

"Quack! Quack! Quack!"

Keith's mummy and all his brothers and sisters had come back to join in with Claude's hooty music!

TOOT! TOOT! TOOT!

"Oh, I do so love a happy ending!" said Sir Bobblysock, dabbing his eyes with his nice lace hanky.

A-ROOTY-TOOTY-TOOTUM!
TA-TOOTY-TOOT-TOOT!

Claude led everyone in a big parade – all the way to Pawhaven park!

"Well done!" said Benny Begonia. He was very impressed with Claude and asked if he wouldn't mind being the park's Chief Duck Minder.

"I'd love to," said Claude, "but I think Sir Bobblysock
needs some peace and quiet after all that noise."

"My nerves are all of a jangle," swooned Sir Bobblysock.

Just then, they were startled by a very familiar noise . . .

"WAAAAAAAAAH!!!"

Oh dear.
Keith didn't want Claude to go.

"Keith likes you, Claude," said Sir Bobbysock, panicking. "He doesn't want you to leave. What are we going to do now?"

Luckily, Claude knew just what to do . . .

When Mr and Mrs Shinyshoes, the nice people who also lived in Claude's house, returned home that evening, they were surprised to find a family of ducks swimming in the kitchen sink.

"Goodness me!" said Mr Shinyshoes. "Where have all these ducks come from?"

TOOT

"You don't suppose Claude
knows anything about it,
do you?" asked Mrs Shinyshoes.

"Of course not, dear," said
Mr Shinyshoes. "Claude's been
fast asleep all day."

But Claude did know something about it.
And we do too, don't we?

HODDER CHILDREN'S BOOKS

First Published in Great Britain in 2019
by Hodder and Stoughton

1 3 5 7 9 10 8 6 4 2

Based on the original 'Claude' series
published by Hodder Children's Books,
written and illustrated by Alex T. Smith

Storybook text written by Davey Moore

Copyright in images and script for
All About Keith written by Alex T. Smith
© 2019 Sixteen South Limited

All rights reserved

A CIP catalogue record for this book
is available from the British Library.

ISBN 978 1 444 93860 9

Printed and bound in China

Hodder Children's Books
An imprint of Hachette Children's Group
Part of Hodder and Stoughton
Carmelite House
50 Victoria Embankment
London, EC4Y 0DZ

An Hachette UK Company
www.hachette.co.uk
www.hachettechildrens.co.uk

FSC
MIX
Paper from
responsible sources
FSC® C104740
www.fsc.org